A MIDSUMMER NIGHT'S DREAM

by William Shakespeare

Disclaimer

The views of the reader do not necessarily reflect the opinions, beliefs and views expressed by the author.

The author and publisher disclaim all liability in connection with the use of the information contained in this book.

CONTENTS

Dramatis Personæ

THESEUS, Duke of Athens
HIPPOLYTA, Queen of the Amazons, bethrothed to Theseus
EGEUS, Father to Hermia
HERMIA, daughter to Egeus, in love with Lysander
HELENA, in love with Demetrius
LYSANDER, in love with Hermia
DEMETRIUS, in love with Hermia
PHILOSTRATE, Master of the Revels to Theseus

QUINCE, the Carpenter
SNUG, the Joiner
BOTTOM, the Weaver
FLUTE, the Bellows-mender
SNOUT, the Tinker
STARVELING, the Tailor

OBERON, King of the Fairies
TITANIA, Queen of the Fairies
PUCK, or ROBIN GOODFELLOW, a Fairy
PEASEBLOSSOM, Fairy
COBWEB, Fairy
MOTH, Fairy
MUSTARDSEED, Fairy

PYRAMUS, THISBE, WALL, MOONSHINE, LION; Characters in the Interlude performed by the Clowns

Other Fairies attending their King and Queen
Attendants on Theseus and Hippolyta
SCENE: Athens, and a wood not far from it

ACT I

SCENE I.
Athens. A room in the Palace of Theseus

Enter Theseus, Hippolyta, Philostrate and Attendants.
THESEUS.
Now, fair Hippolyta, our nuptial hour
Draws on apace; four happy days bring in
Another moon; but oh, methinks, how slow
This old moon wanes! She lingers my desires,
Like to a step-dame or a dowager,
Long withering out a young man's revenue.
HIPPOLYTA.
Four days will quickly steep themselves in night;
Four nights will quickly dream away the time;
And then the moon, like to a silver bow
New bent in heaven, shall behold the night
Of our solemnities.
THESEUS.
Go, Philostrate,
Stir up the Athenian youth to merriments;
Awake the pert and nimble spirit of mirth;
Turn melancholy forth to funerals;
The pale companion is not for our pomp.
[Exit Philostrate.]
Hippolyta, I woo'd thee with my sword,
And won thy love doing thee injuries;
But I will wed thee in another key,
With pomp, with triumph, and with revelling.
Enter Egeus, Hermia, Lysander and Demetrius.

EGEUS.
Happy be Theseus, our renownèd Duke!
THESEUS.
Thanks, good Egeus. What's the news with thee?
EGEUS.
Full of vexation come I, with complaint
Against my child, my daughter Hermia.
Stand forth, Demetrius. My noble lord,
This man hath my consent to marry her.
Stand forth, Lysander. And, my gracious Duke,
This man hath bewitch'd the bosom of my child.
Thou, thou, Lysander, thou hast given her rhymes,
And interchang'd love-tokens with my child.
Thou hast by moonlight at her window sung,
With feigning voice, verses of feigning love;
And stol'n the impression of her fantasy
With bracelets of thy hair, rings, gauds, conceits,
Knacks, trifles, nosegays, sweetmeats (messengers
Of strong prevailment in unharden'd youth)
With cunning hast thou filch'd my daughter's heart,
Turn'd her obedience (which is due to me)
To stubborn harshness. And, my gracious Duke,
Be it so she will not here before your grace
Consent to marry with Demetrius,
I beg the ancient privilege of Athens:
As she is mine I may dispose of her;
Which shall be either to this gentleman
Or to her death, according to our law
Immediately provided in that case.
THESEUS.
What say you, Hermia? Be advis'd, fair maid.
To you your father should be as a god;
One that compos'd your beauties, yea, and one
To whom you are but as a form in wax
By him imprinted, and within his power

To leave the figure, or disfigure it.
Demetrius is a worthy gentleman.
HERMIA.
So is Lysander.
THESEUS.
In himself he is.
But in this kind, wanting your father's voice,
The other must be held the worthier.
HERMIA.
I would my father look'd but with my eyes.
THESEUS.
Rather your eyes must with his judgment look.
HERMIA.
I do entreat your Grace to pardon me.
I know not by what power I am made bold,
Nor how it may concern my modesty
In such a presence here to plead my thoughts:
But I beseech your Grace that I may know
The worst that may befall me in this case,
If I refuse to wed Demetrius.
THESEUS.
Either to die the death, or to abjure
For ever the society of men.
Therefore, fair Hermia, question your desires,
Know of your youth, examine well your blood,
Whether, if you yield not to your father's choice,
You can endure the livery of a nun,
For aye to be in shady cloister mew'd,
To live a barren sister all your life,
Chanting faint hymns to the cold fruitless moon.
Thrice-blessèd they that master so their blood
To undergo such maiden pilgrimage,
But earthlier happy is the rose distill'd
Than that which, withering on the virgin thorn,
Grows, lives, and dies, in single blessedness.

HERMIA.
So will I grow, so live, so die, my lord,
Ere I will yield my virgin patent up
Unto his lordship, whose unwishèd yoke
My soul consents not to give sovereignty.
THESEUS.
Take time to pause; and by the next new moon
The sealing-day betwixt my love and me
For everlasting bond of fellowship,
Upon that day either prepare to die
For disobedience to your father's will,
Or else to wed Demetrius, as he would,
Or on Diana's altar to protest
For aye austerity and single life.
DEMETRIUS.
Relent, sweet Hermia; and, Lysander, yield
Thy crazèd title to my certain right.
LYSANDER.
You have her father's love, Demetrius.
Let me have Hermia's. Do you marry him.
EGEUS.
Scornful Lysander, true, he hath my love;
And what is mine my love shall render him;
And she is mine, and all my right of her
I do estate unto Demetrius.
LYSANDER.
I am, my lord, as well deriv'd as he,
As well possess'd; my love is more than his;
My fortunes every way as fairly rank'd,
If not with vantage, as Demetrius';
And, which is more than all these boasts can be,
I am belov'd of beauteous Hermia.
Why should not I then prosecute my right?
Demetrius, I'll avouch it to his head,
Made love to Nedar's daughter, Helena,

And won her soul; and she, sweet lady, dotes,
Devoutly dotes, dotes in idolatry,
Upon this spotted and inconstant man.
THESEUS.
I must confess that I have heard so much,
And with Demetrius thought to have spoke thereof;
But, being over-full of self-affairs,
My mind did lose it.—But, Demetrius, come,
And come, Egeus; you shall go with me.
I have some private schooling for you both.—
For you, fair Hermia, look you arm yourself
To fit your fancies to your father's will,
Or else the law of Athens yields you up
(Which by no means we may extenuate)
To death, or to a vow of single life.
Come, my Hippolyta. What cheer, my love?
Demetrius and Egeus, go along;
I must employ you in some business
Against our nuptial, and confer with you
Of something nearly that concerns yourselves.
EGEUS.
With duty and desire we follow you.
[Exeunt all but Lysander and Hermia.]
LYSANDER.
How now, my love? Why is your cheek so pale?
How chance the roses there do fade so fast?
HERMIA.
Belike for want of rain, which I could well
Beteem them from the tempest of my eyes.
LYSANDER.
Ay me! For aught that I could ever read,
Could ever hear by tale or history,
The course of true love never did run smooth.
But either it was different in blood—

HERMIA.
O cross! Too high to be enthrall'd to low.
LYSANDER.
Or else misgraffèd in respect of years—
HERMIA.
O spite! Too old to be engag'd to young.
LYSANDER.
Or else it stood upon the choice of friends—
HERMIA.
O hell! to choose love by another's eyes!
LYSANDER.
Or, if there were a sympathy in choice,
War, death, or sickness did lay siege to it,
Making it momentany as a sound,
Swift as a shadow, short as any dream,
Brief as the lightning in the collied night
That, in a spleen, unfolds both heaven and earth,
And, ere a man hath power to say, 'Behold!'
The jaws of darkness do devour it up:
So quick bright things come to confusion.
HERMIA.
If then true lovers have ever cross'd,
It stands as an edict in destiny.
Then let us teach our trial patience,
Because it is a customary cross,
As due to love as thoughts and dreams and sighs,
Wishes and tears, poor fancy's followers.
LYSANDER.
A good persuasion; therefore, hear me, Hermia.
I have a widow aunt, a dowager
Of great revenue, and she hath no child.
From Athens is her house remote seven leagues,
And she respects me as her only son.
There, gentle Hermia, may I marry thee,
And to that place the sharp Athenian law

Cannot pursue us. If thou lovest me then,
Steal forth thy father's house tomorrow night;
And in the wood, a league without the town
(Where I did meet thee once with Helena
To do observance to a morn of May),
There will I stay for thee.
HERMIA.
My good Lysander!
I swear to thee by Cupid's strongest bow,
By his best arrow with the golden head,
By the simplicity of Venus' doves,
By that which knitteth souls and prospers loves,
And by that fire which burn'd the Carthage queen
When the false Trojan under sail was seen,
By all the vows that ever men have broke
(In number more than ever women spoke),
In that same place thou hast appointed me,
Tomorrow truly will I meet with thee.
LYSANDER.
Keep promise, love. Look, here comes Helena.
Enter Helena.
HERMIA.
God speed fair Helena! Whither away?
HELENA.
Call you me fair? That fair again unsay.
Demetrius loves your fair. O happy fair!
Your eyes are lode-stars and your tongue's sweet air
More tuneable than lark to shepherd's ear,
When wheat is green, when hawthorn buds appear.
Sickness is catching. O were favour so,
Yours would I catch, fair Hermia, ere I go.
My ear should catch your voice, my eye your eye,
My tongue should catch your tongue's sweet melody.
Were the world mine, Demetrius being bated,
The rest I'd give to be to you translated.

O, teach me how you look, and with what art
You sway the motion of Demetrius' heart!
HERMIA.
I frown upon him, yet he loves me still.
HELENA.
O that your frowns would teach my smiles such skill!
HERMIA.
I give him curses, yet he gives me love.
HELENA.
O that my prayers could such affection move!
HERMIA.
The more I hate, the more he follows me.
HELENA.
The more I love, the more he hateth me.
HERMIA.
His folly, Helena, is no fault of mine.
HELENA.
None but your beauty; would that fault were mine!
HERMIA.
Take comfort: he no more shall see my face;
Lysander and myself will fly this place.
Before the time I did Lysander see,
Seem'd Athens as a paradise to me.
O, then, what graces in my love do dwell,
That he hath turn'd a heaven into hell!
LYSANDER.
Helen, to you our minds we will unfold:
Tomorrow night, when Phoebe doth behold
Her silver visage in the watery glass,
Decking with liquid pearl the bladed grass
(A time that lovers' flights doth still conceal),
Through Athens' gates have we devis'd to steal.
HERMIA.
And in the wood where often you and I
Upon faint primrose beds were wont to lie,

Emptying our bosoms of their counsel sweet,
There my Lysander and myself shall meet,
And thence from Athens turn away our eyes,
To seek new friends and stranger companies.
Farewell, sweet playfellow. Pray thou for us,
And good luck grant thee thy Demetrius!
Keep word, Lysander. We must starve our sight
From lovers' food, till morrow deep midnight.
LYSANDER.
I will, my Hermia.
[Exit Hermia.]
Helena, adieu.
As you on him, Demetrius dote on you!
[Exit Lysander.]
HELENA.
How happy some o'er other some can be!
Through Athens I am thought as fair as she.
But what of that? Demetrius thinks not so;
He will not know what all but he do know.
And as he errs, doting on Hermia's eyes,
So I, admiring of his qualities.
Things base and vile, holding no quantity,
Love can transpose to form and dignity.
Love looks not with the eyes, but with the mind;
And therefore is wing'd Cupid painted blind.
Nor hath love's mind of any judgment taste.
Wings, and no eyes, figure unheedy haste.
And therefore is love said to be a child,
Because in choice he is so oft beguil'd.
As waggish boys in game themselves forswear,
So the boy Love is perjur'd everywhere.
For, ere Demetrius look'd on Hermia's eyne,
He hail'd down oaths that he was only mine;
And when this hail some heat from Hermia felt,
So he dissolv'd, and showers of oaths did melt.

I will go tell him of fair Hermia's flight.
Then to the wood will he tomorrow night
Pursue her; and for this intelligence
If I have thanks, it is a dear expense.
But herein mean I to enrich my pain,
To have his sight thither and back again.
[Exit Helena.]

SCENE II.
The Same. A Room in a Cottage

Enter Quince, Snug, Bottom, Flute, Snout and Starveling.
QUINCE.
Is all our company here?
BOTTOM.
You were best to call them generally, man by man, according to the scrip.
QUINCE.
Here is the scroll of every man's name, which is thought fit through all Athens, to play in our interlude before the Duke and Duchess, on his wedding-day at night.
BOTTOM.
First, good Peter Quince, say what the play treats on; then read the names of the actors; and so grow to a point.
QUINCE.
Marry, our play is The most lamentable comedy and most cruel death of Pyramus and Thisbe.
BOTTOM.
A very good piece of work, I assure you, and a merry. Now, good Peter Quince, call forth your actors by the scroll. Masters, spread yourselves.
QUINCE.
Answer, as I call you. Nick Bottom, the weaver.
BOTTOM.
Ready. Name what part I am for, and proceed.
QUINCE.
You, Nick Bottom, are set down for Pyramus.
BOTTOM.
What is Pyramus—a lover, or a tyrant?
QUINCE.
A lover, that kills himself most gallantly for love.
BOTTOM.
That will ask some tears in the true performing of it. If I do it, let the audience look to their eyes. I will move storms; I will condole in some measure. To the rest—yet my chief humour is for a tyrant. I could play

Ercles rarely, or a part to tear a cat in, to make all split.

The raging rocks
And shivering shocks
Shall break the locks
    Of prison gates,
And Phibbus' car
Shall shine from far,
And make and mar
    The foolish Fates.

This was lofty. Now name the rest of the players. This is Ercles' vein, a tyrant's vein; a lover is more condoling.
QUINCE.
Francis Flute, the bellows-mender.
FLUTE.
Here, Peter Quince.
QUINCE.
Flute, you must take Thisbe on you.
FLUTE.
What is Thisbe? A wandering knight?
QUINCE.
It is the lady that Pyramus must love.
FLUTE.
Nay, faith, let not me play a woman. I have a beard coming.
QUINCE.
That's all one. You shall play it in a mask, and you may speak as small as you will.
BOTTOM.
And I may hide my face, let me play Thisbe too. I'll speak in a monstrous little voice; 'Thisne, Thisne!'—'Ah, Pyramus, my lover dear! thy Thisbe dear! and lady dear!'
QUINCE.
No, no, you must play Pyramus; and, Flute, you Thisbe.

BOTTOM.
Well, proceed.
QUINCE.
Robin Starveling, the tailor.
STARVELING.
Here, Peter Quince.
QUINCE.
Robin Starveling, you must play Thisbe's mother.
Tom Snout, the tinker.
SNOUT
Here, Peter Quince.
QUINCE.
You, Pyramus' father; myself, Thisbe's father;
Snug, the joiner, you, the lion's part. And, I hope here is a play fitted.
SNUG
Have you the lion's part written? Pray you, if it be, give it me, for I am slow of study.
QUINCE.
You may do it extempore, for it is nothing but roaring.
BOTTOM.
Let me play the lion too. I will roar that I will do any man's heart good to hear me. I will roar that I will make the Duke say 'Let him roar again, let him roar again.'
QUINCE.
If you should do it too terribly, you would fright the Duchess and the ladies, that they would shriek; and that were enough to hang us all.
ALL
That would hang us every mother's son.
BOTTOM.
I grant you, friends, if you should fright the ladies out of their wits, they would have no more discretion but to hang us. But I will aggravate my voice so, that I will roar you as gently as any sucking dove; I will roar you an 'twere any nightingale.
QUINCE.
You can play no part but Pyramus, for Pyramus is a sweet-faced man; a

proper man as one shall see in a summer's day; a most lovely gentleman-like man. Therefore you must needs play Pyramus.

BOTTOM.

Well, I will undertake it. What beard were I best to play it in?

QUINCE.

Why, what you will.

BOTTOM.

I will discharge it in either your straw-colour beard, your orange-tawny beard, your purple-in-grain beard, or your French-crown-colour beard, your perfect yellow.

QUINCE.

Some of your French crowns have no hair at all, and then you will play bare-faced. But, masters, here are your parts, and I am to entreat you, request you, and desire you, to con them by tomorrow night; and meet me in the palace wood, a mile without the town, by moonlight; there will we rehearse, for if we meet in the city, we shall be dogg'd with company, and our devices known. In the meantime I will draw a bill of properties, such as our play wants. I pray you fail me not.

BOTTOM.

We will meet, and there we may rehearse most obscenely and courageously. Take pains, be perfect; adieu.

QUINCE.

At the Duke's oak we meet.

BOTTOM.

Enough. Hold, or cut bow-strings.

[Exeunt.]

ACT II

SCENE I.
A wood near Athens

Enter a Fairy at one door, and Puck at another.
PUCK.
How now, spirit! Whither wander you?
FAIRY
Over hill, over dale,
Thorough bush, thorough brier,
Over park, over pale,
Thorough flood, thorough fire,
I do wander everywhere,
Swifter than the moon's sphere;
And I serve the Fairy Queen,
To dew her orbs upon the green.
The cowslips tall her pensioners be,
In their gold coats spots you see;
Those be rubies, fairy favours,
In those freckles live their savours.
I must go seek some dew-drops here,
And hang a pearl in every cowslip's ear.
Farewell, thou lob of spirits; I'll be gone.
Our Queen and all her elves come here anon.
PUCK.
The King doth keep his revels here tonight;
Take heed the Queen come not within his sight,
For Oberon is passing fell and wrath,
Because that she, as her attendant, hath
A lovely boy, stol'n from an Indian king;
She never had so sweet a changeling.

And jealous Oberon would have the child
Knight of his train, to trace the forests wild:
But she perforce withholds the lovèd boy,
Crowns him with flowers, and makes him all her joy.
And now they never meet in grove or green,
By fountain clear, or spangled starlight sheen,
But they do square; that all their elves for fear
Creep into acorn cups, and hide them there.
FAIRY
Either I mistake your shape and making quite,
Or else you are that shrewd and knavish sprite
Call'd Robin Goodfellow. Are not you he
That frights the maidens of the villagery,
Skim milk, and sometimes labour in the quern,
And bootless make the breathless housewife churn,
And sometime make the drink to bear no barm,
Mislead night-wanderers, laughing at their harm?
Those that Hobgoblin call you, and sweet Puck,
You do their work, and they shall have good luck.
Are not you he?
PUCK.
Thou speak'st aright;
I am that merry wanderer of the night.
I jest to Oberon, and make him smile,
When I a fat and bean-fed horse beguile,
Neighing in likeness of a filly foal;
And sometime lurk I in a gossip's bowl
In very likeness of a roasted crab,
And, when she drinks, against her lips I bob,
And on her withered dewlap pour the ale.
The wisest aunt, telling the saddest tale,
Sometime for three-foot stool mistaketh me;
Then slip I from her bum, down topples she,
And 'tailor' cries, and falls into a cough;
And then the whole quire hold their hips and loffe

And waxen in their mirth, and neeze, and swear
A merrier hour was never wasted there.
But room, fairy. Here comes Oberon.
FAIRY
And here my mistress. Would that he were gone!
Enter Oberon at one door, with his Train, and Titania at another, with hers.
OBERON.
Ill met by moonlight, proud Titania.
TITANIA.
What, jealous Oberon! Fairies, skip hence;
I have forsworn his bed and company.
OBERON.
Tarry, rash wanton; am not I thy lord?
TITANIA.
Then I must be thy lady; but I know
When thou hast stol'n away from fairyland,
And in the shape of Corin sat all day
Playing on pipes of corn, and versing love
To amorous Phillida. Why art thou here,
Come from the farthest steep of India,
But that, forsooth, the bouncing Amazon,
Your buskin'd mistress and your warrior love,
To Theseus must be wedded; and you come
To give their bed joy and prosperity?
OBERON.
How canst thou thus, for shame, Titania,
Glance at my credit with Hippolyta,
Knowing I know thy love to Theseus?
Didst not thou lead him through the glimmering night
From Perigenia, whom he ravished?
And make him with fair Aegles break his faith,
With Ariadne and Antiopa?
TITANIA.
These are the forgeries of jealousy:
And never, since the middle summer's spring,

Met we on hill, in dale, forest, or mead,
By pavèd fountain, or by rushy brook,
Or on the beachèd margent of the sea,
To dance our ringlets to the whistling wind,
But with thy brawls thou hast disturb'd our sport.
Therefore the winds, piping to us in vain,
As in revenge, have suck'd up from the sea
Contagious fogs; which, falling in the land,
Hath every pelting river made so proud
That they have overborne their continents.
The ox hath therefore stretch'd his yoke in vain,
The ploughman lost his sweat, and the green corn
Hath rotted ere his youth attain'd a beard.
The fold stands empty in the drownèd field,
And crows are fatted with the murrion flock;
The nine-men's-morris is fill'd up with mud,
And the quaint mazes in the wanton green,
For lack of tread, are undistinguishable.
The human mortals want their winter here.
No night is now with hymn or carol blest.
Therefore the moon, the governess of floods,
Pale in her anger, washes all the air,
That rheumatic diseases do abound.
And thorough this distemperature we see
The seasons alter: hoary-headed frosts
Fall in the fresh lap of the crimson rose;
And on old Hiems' thin and icy crown
An odorous chaplet of sweet summer buds
Is, as in mockery, set. The spring, the summer,
The childing autumn, angry winter, change
Their wonted liveries; and the mazed world,
By their increase, now knows not which is which.
And this same progeny of evils comes
From our debate, from our dissension;
We are their parents and original.

OBERON.
Do you amend it, then. It lies in you.
Why should Titania cross her Oberon?
I do but beg a little changeling boy
To be my henchman.
TITANIA.
Set your heart at rest;
The fairyland buys not the child of me.
His mother was a vot'ress of my order,
And in the spicèd Indian air, by night,
Full often hath she gossip'd by my side;
And sat with me on Neptune's yellow sands,
Marking th' embarkèd traders on the flood,
When we have laugh'd to see the sails conceive,
And grow big-bellied with the wanton wind;
Which she, with pretty and with swimming gait
Following (her womb then rich with my young squire),
Would imitate, and sail upon the land,
To fetch me trifles, and return again,
As from a voyage, rich with merchandise.
But she, being mortal, of that boy did die;
And for her sake do I rear up her boy,
And for her sake I will not part with him.
OBERON.
How long within this wood intend you stay?
TITANIA.
Perchance till after Theseus' wedding-day.
If you will patiently dance in our round,
And see our moonlight revels, go with us;
If not, shun me, and I will spare your haunts.
OBERON.
Give me that boy and I will go with thee.
TITANIA.
Not for thy fairy kingdom. Fairies, away.
We shall chide downright if I longer stay.

[Exit Titania with her Train.]
OBERON.
Well, go thy way. Thou shalt not from this grove
Till I torment thee for this injury.—
My gentle Puck, come hither. Thou rememb'rest
Since once I sat upon a promontory,
And heard a mermaid on a dolphin's back
Uttering such dulcet and harmonious breath
That the rude sea grew civil at her song
And certain stars shot madly from their spheres
To hear the sea-maid's music.
PUCK.
I remember.
OBERON.
That very time I saw, (but thou couldst not),
Flying between the cold moon and the earth,
Cupid all arm'd: a certain aim he took
At a fair vestal, thronèd by the west,
And loos'd his love-shaft smartly from his bow
As it should pierce a hundred thousand hearts.
But I might see young Cupid's fiery shaft
Quench'd in the chaste beams of the watery moon;
And the imperial votress passed on,
In maiden meditation, fancy-free.
Yet mark'd I where the bolt of Cupid fell:
It fell upon a little western flower,
Before milk-white, now purple with love's wound,
And maidens call it love-in-idleness.
Fetch me that flower, the herb I showed thee once:
The juice of it on sleeping eyelids laid
Will make or man or woman madly dote
Upon the next live creature that it sees.
Fetch me this herb, and be thou here again
Ere the leviathan can swim a league.

PUCK.
I'll put a girdle round about the earth
In forty minutes.
[Exit Puck.]
OBERON.
Having once this juice,
I'll watch Titania when she is asleep,
And drop the liquor of it in her eyes:
The next thing then she waking looks upon
(Be it on lion, bear, or wolf, or bull,
On meddling monkey, or on busy ape)
She shall pursue it with the soul of love.
And ere I take this charm from off her sight
(As I can take it with another herb)
I'll make her render up her page to me.
But who comes here? I am invisible;
And I will overhear their conference.
Enter Demetrius, Helena following him.
DEMETRIUS.
I love thee not, therefore pursue me not.
Where is Lysander and fair Hermia?
The one I'll slay, the other slayeth me.
Thou told'st me they were stol'n into this wood,
And here am I, and wode within this wood
Because I cannot meet with Hermia.
Hence, get thee gone, and follow me no more.
HELENA.
You draw me, you hard-hearted adamant,
But yet you draw not iron, for my heart
Is true as steel. Leave you your power to draw,
And I shall have no power to follow you.
DEMETRIUS.
Do I entice you? Do I speak you fair?
Or rather do I not in plainest truth
Tell you I do not, nor I cannot love you?

HELENA.
And even for that do I love you the more.
I am your spaniel; and, Demetrius,
The more you beat me, I will fawn on you.
Use me but as your spaniel, spurn me, strike me,
Neglect me, lose me; only give me leave,
Unworthy as I am, to follow you.
What worser place can I beg in your love,
(And yet a place of high respect with me)
Than to be usèd as you use your dog?
DEMETRIUS.
Tempt not too much the hatred of my spirit;
For I am sick when I do look on thee.
HELENA.
And I am sick when I look not on you.
DEMETRIUS.
You do impeach your modesty too much
To leave the city and commit yourself
Into the hands of one that loves you not,
To trust the opportunity of night
And the ill counsel of a desert place,
With the rich worth of your virginity.
HELENA.
Your virtue is my privilege: for that
It is not night when I do see your face,
Therefore I think I am not in the night;
Nor doth this wood lack worlds of company,
For you, in my respect, are all the world.
Then how can it be said I am alone
When all the world is here to look on me?
DEMETRIUS.
I'll run from thee and hide me in the brakes,
And leave thee to the mercy of wild beasts.
HELENA.
The wildest hath not such a heart as you.

Run when you will, the story shall be chang'd;
Apollo flies, and Daphne holds the chase;
The dove pursues the griffin, the mild hind
Makes speed to catch the tiger. Bootless speed,
When cowardice pursues and valour flies!
DEMETRIUS.
I will not stay thy questions. Let me go,
Or if thou follow me, do not believe
But I shall do thee mischief in the wood.
HELENA.
Ay, in the temple, in the town, the field,
You do me mischief. Fie, Demetrius!
Your wrongs do set a scandal on my sex.
We cannot fight for love as men may do.
We should be woo'd, and were not made to woo.
[Exit Demetrius.]
I'll follow thee, and make a heaven of hell,
To die upon the hand I love so well.
[Exit Helena.]
OBERON.
Fare thee well, nymph. Ere he do leave this grove,
Thou shalt fly him, and he shall seek thy love.
Enter Puck.
Hast thou the flower there? Welcome, wanderer.
PUCK.
Ay, there it is.
OBERON.
I pray thee give it me.
I know a bank where the wild thyme blows,
Where oxlips and the nodding violet grows,
Quite over-canopied with luscious woodbine,
With sweet musk-roses, and with eglantine.
There sleeps Titania sometime of the night,
Lull'd in these flowers with dances and delight;
And there the snake throws her enamell'd skin,

Weed wide enough to wrap a fairy in.
And with the juice of this I'll streak her eyes,
And make her full of hateful fantasies.
Take thou some of it, and seek through this grove:
A sweet Athenian lady is in love
With a disdainful youth. Anoint his eyes;
But do it when the next thing he espies
May be the lady. Thou shalt know the man
By the Athenian garments he hath on.
Effect it with some care, that he may prove
More fond on her than she upon her love:
And look thou meet me ere the first cock crow.
PUCK.
Fear not, my lord, your servant shall do so.
[Exeunt.]

SCENE II.
Another part of the wood

Enter Titania with her Train.
TITANIA.
Come, now a roundel and a fairy song;
Then for the third part of a minute, hence;
Some to kill cankers in the musk-rose buds;
Some war with reremice for their leathern wings,
To make my small elves coats; and some keep back
The clamorous owl, that nightly hoots and wonders
At our quaint spirits. Sing me now asleep;
Then to your offices, and let me rest.
Fairies sing.
FIRST FAIRY.
You spotted snakes with double tongue,
Thorny hedgehogs, be not seen;
Newts and blind-worms do no wrong,
Come not near our Fairy Queen:
CHORUS.
Philomel, with melody,
Sing in our sweet lullaby:
Lulla, lulla, lullaby; lulla, lulla, lullaby.
Never harm, nor spell, nor charm,
Come our lovely lady nigh;
So good night, with lullaby.
FIRST FAIRY.
Weaving spiders, come not here;
Hence, you long-legg'd spinners, hence.
Beetles black, approach not near;
Worm nor snail do no offence.
CHORUS.
Philomel with melody, &c.

SECOND FAIRY.
Hence away! Now all is well.
One aloof stand sentinel.
[Exeunt Fairies. Titania sleeps.]
Enter Oberon.
OBERON.
What thou seest when thou dost wake,
[Squeezes the flower on Titania's eyelids.]
Do it for thy true love take;
Love and languish for his sake.
Be it ounce, or cat, or bear,
Pard, or boar with bristled hair,
In thy eye that shall appear
When thou wak'st, it is thy dear.
Wake when some vile thing is near.
[Exit.]
Enter Lysander and Hermia.
LYSANDER.
Fair love, you faint with wand'ring in the wood.
And, to speak troth, I have forgot our way.
We'll rest us, Hermia, if you think it good,
And tarry for the comfort of the day.
HERMIA.
Be it so, Lysander: find you out a bed,
For I upon this bank will rest my head.
LYSANDER.
One turf shall serve as pillow for us both;
One heart, one bed, two bosoms, and one troth.
HERMIA.
Nay, good Lysander; for my sake, my dear,
Lie further off yet, do not lie so near.
LYSANDER.
O take the sense, sweet, of my innocence!
Love takes the meaning in love's conference.
I mean that my heart unto yours is knit,

So that but one heart we can make of it:
Two bosoms interchainèd with an oath,
So then two bosoms and a single troth.
Then by your side no bed-room me deny;
For lying so, Hermia, I do not lie.
HERMIA.
Lysander riddles very prettily.
Now much beshrew my manners and my pride,
If Hermia meant to say Lysander lied!
But, gentle friend, for love and courtesy
Lie further off, in human modesty,
Such separation as may well be said
Becomes a virtuous bachelor and a maid,
So far be distant; and good night, sweet friend:
Thy love ne'er alter till thy sweet life end!
LYSANDER.
Amen, amen, to that fair prayer say I;
And then end life when I end loyalty!
Here is my bed. Sleep give thee all his rest!
HERMIA.
With half that wish the wisher's eyes be pressed!
[They sleep.]
Enter Puck.
PUCK.
Through the forest have I gone,
But Athenian found I none,
On whose eyes I might approve
This flower's force in stirring love.
Night and silence! Who is here?
Weeds of Athens he doth wear:
This is he, my master said,
Despisèd the Athenian maid;
And here the maiden, sleeping sound,
On the dank and dirty ground.
Pretty soul, she durst not lie

Near this lack-love, this kill-courtesy.
Churl, upon thy eyes I throw
All the power this charm doth owe;
When thou wak'st let love forbid
Sleep his seat on thy eyelid.
So awake when I am gone;
For I must now to Oberon.
[Exit.]
Enter Demetrius and Helena, running.
HELENA.
Stay, though thou kill me, sweet Demetrius.
DEMETRIUS.
I charge thee, hence, and do not haunt me thus.
HELENA.
O, wilt thou darkling leave me? Do not so.
DEMETRIUS.
Stay, on thy peril; I alone will go.
[Exit Demetrius.]
HELENA.
O, I am out of breath in this fond chase!
The more my prayer, the lesser is my grace.
Happy is Hermia, wheresoe'er she lies,
For she hath blessèd and attractive eyes.
How came her eyes so bright? Not with salt tears.
If so, my eyes are oftener wash'd than hers.
No, no, I am as ugly as a bear,
For beasts that meet me run away for fear:
Therefore no marvel though Demetrius
Do, as a monster, fly my presence thus.
What wicked and dissembling glass of mine
Made me compare with Hermia's sphery eyne?
But who is here? Lysander, on the ground!
Dead or asleep? I see no blood, no wound.
Lysander, if you live, good sir, awake.

LYSANDER.
[Waking.] And run through fire I will for thy sweet sake.
Transparent Helena! Nature shows art,
That through thy bosom makes me see thy heart.
Where is Demetrius? O, how fit a word
Is that vile name to perish on my sword!
HELENA.
Do not say so, Lysander, say not so.
What though he love your Hermia? Lord, what though?
Yet Hermia still loves you. Then be content.
LYSANDER.
Content with Hermia? No, I do repent
The tedious minutes I with her have spent.
Not Hermia, but Helena I love.
Who will not change a raven for a dove?
The will of man is by his reason sway'd,
And reason says you are the worthier maid.
Things growing are not ripe until their season;
So I, being young, till now ripe not to reason;
And touching now the point of human skill,
Reason becomes the marshal to my will,
And leads me to your eyes, where I o'erlook
Love's stories, written in love's richest book.
HELENA.
Wherefore was I to this keen mockery born?
When at your hands did I deserve this scorn?
Is't not enough, is't not enough, young man,
That I did never, no, nor never can
Deserve a sweet look from Demetrius' eye,
But you must flout my insufficiency?
Good troth, you do me wrong, good sooth, you do,
In such disdainful manner me to woo.
But fare you well; perforce I must confess,
I thought you lord of more true gentleness.

O, that a lady of one man refus'd,
Should of another therefore be abus'd!
[Exit.]
LYSANDER.
She sees not Hermia. Hermia, sleep thou there,
And never mayst thou come Lysander near!
For, as a surfeit of the sweetest things
The deepest loathing to the stomach brings;
Or as the heresies that men do leave
Are hated most of those they did deceive;
So thou, my surfeit and my heresy,
Of all be hated, but the most of me!
And, all my powers, address your love and might
To honour Helen, and to be her knight!
[Exit.]
HERMIA.
[Starting.] Help me, Lysander, help me! Do thy best
To pluck this crawling serpent from my breast!
Ay me, for pity! What a dream was here!
Lysander, look how I do quake with fear.
Methought a serpent eat my heart away,
And you sat smiling at his cruel prey.
Lysander! What, removed? Lysander! lord!
What, out of hearing? Gone? No sound, no word?
Alack, where are you? Speak, and if you hear;
Speak, of all loves! I swoon almost with fear.
No? Then I well perceive you are not nigh.
Either death or you I'll find immediately.
[Exit.]

ACT III

SCENE I.
The Wood.

The Queen of Fairies still lying asleep.
Enter Bottom, Quince, Snout, Starveling, Snug and Flute.
BOTTOM.
Are we all met?
QUINCE.
Pat, pat; and here's a marvellous convenient place for our rehearsal. This green plot shall be our stage, this hawthorn brake our tiring-house; and we will do it in action, as we will do it before the Duke.
BOTTOM.
Peter Quince?
QUINCE.
What sayest thou, bully Bottom?
BOTTOM.
There are things in this comedy of Pyramus and Thisbe that will never please. First, Pyramus must draw a sword to kill himself; which the ladies cannot abide. How answer you that?
SNOUT
By'r lakin, a parlous fear.
STARVELING.
I believe we must leave the killing out, when all is done.
BOTTOM.
Not a whit; I have a device to make all well. Write me a prologue, and let the prologue seem to say we will do no harm with our swords, and that Pyramus is not killed indeed; and for the more better assurance, tell them that I Pyramus am not Pyramus but Bottom the weaver. This will put them out of fear.

QUINCE.
Well, we will have such a prologue; and it shall be written in eight and six.
BOTTOM.
No, make it two more; let it be written in eight and eight.
SNOUT
Will not the ladies be afeard of the lion?
STARVELING.
I fear it, I promise you.
BOTTOM.
Masters, you ought to consider with yourselves, to bring in (God shield us!) a lion among ladies is a most dreadful thing. For there is not a more fearful wild-fowl than your lion living; and we ought to look to it.
SNOUT
Therefore another prologue must tell he is not a lion.
BOTTOM.
Nay, you must name his name, and half his face must be seen through the lion's neck; and he himself must speak through, saying thus, or to the same defect: 'Ladies,' or, 'Fair ladies, I would wish you,' or, 'I would request you,' or, 'I would entreat you, not to fear, not to tremble: my life for yours. If you think I come hither as a lion, it were pity of my life. No, I am no such thing; I am a man as other men are': and there, indeed, let him name his name, and tell them plainly he is Snug the joiner.
QUINCE.
Well, it shall be so. But there is two hard things: that is, to bring the moonlight into a chamber, for you know, Pyramus and Thisbe meet by moonlight.
SNOUT
Doth the moon shine that night we play our play?
BOTTOM.
A calendar, a calendar! Look in the almanack; find out moonshine, find out moonshine.
QUINCE.
Yes, it doth shine that night.

BOTTOM.

Why, then may you leave a casement of the great chamber window, where we play, open; and the moon may shine in at the casement.

QUINCE.

Ay; or else one must come in with a bush of thorns and a lantern, and say he comes to disfigure or to present the person of Moonshine. Then there is another thing: we must have a wall in the great chamber; for Pyramus and Thisbe, says the story, did talk through the chink of a wall.

SNOUT

You can never bring in a wall. What say you, Bottom?

BOTTOM.

Some man or other must present Wall. And let him have some plaster, or some loam, or some rough-cast about him, to signify wall; and let him hold his fingers thus, and through that cranny shall Pyramus and Thisbe whisper.

QUINCE.

If that may be, then all is well. Come, sit down, every mother's son, and rehearse your parts. Pyramus, you begin: when you have spoken your speech, enter into that brake; and so everyone according to his cue.

Enter Puck behind.

PUCK.

What hempen homespuns have we swaggering here,
So near the cradle of the Fairy Queen?
What, a play toward? I'll be an auditor;
An actor too perhaps, if I see cause.

QUINCE.

Speak, Pyramus.—Thisbe, stand forth.

PYRAMUS.

Thisbe, the flowers of odious savours sweet

QUINCE.

Odours, odours.

PYRAMUS.

. . . odours savours sweet.
So hath thy breath, my dearest Thisbe dear.
But hark, a voice! Stay thou but here awhile,
And by and by I will to thee appear.

[Exit.]
PUCK.
A stranger Pyramus than e'er played here!
[Exit.]
THISBE.
Must I speak now?
QUINCE.
Ay, marry, must you, For you must understand he goes but to see a noise that he heard, and is to come again.
THISBE.
Most radiant Pyramus, most lily-white of hue,
Of colour like the red rose on triumphant brier,
Most brisky juvenal, and eke most lovely Jew,
As true as truest horse, that yet would never tire,
I'll meet thee, Pyramus, at Ninny's tomb.
QUINCE.
Ninus' tomb, man! Why, you must not speak that yet. That you answer to Pyramus. You speak all your part at once, cues, and all.—Pyramus enter! Your cue is past; it is 'never tire.'
THISBE.
O, As true as truest horse, that yet would never tire.
Enter Puck and Bottom with an ass's head.
PYRAMUS.
If I were fair, Thisbe, I were only thine.
QUINCE.
O monstrous! O strange! We are haunted. Pray, masters, fly, masters! Help!
[Exeunt Clowns.]
PUCK.
I'll follow you. I'll lead you about a round,
  Through bog, through bush, through brake, through brier;
Sometime a horse I'll be, sometime a hound,
  A hog, a headless bear, sometime a fire;
And neigh, and bark, and grunt, and roar, and burn,
Like horse, hound, hog, bear, fire, at every turn.
[Exit.]

BOTTOM.
Why do they run away? This is a knavery of them to make me afeard.
Enter Snout.
SNOUT
O Bottom, thou art changed! What do I see on thee?
BOTTOM.
What do you see? You see an ass-head of your own, do you?
[Exit Snout.]
Enter Quince.
QUINCE.
Bless thee, Bottom! bless thee! Thou art translated.
[Exit.]
BOTTOM.
I see their knavery. This is to make an ass of me, to fright me, if they could. But I will not stir from this place, do what they can. I will walk up and down here, and I will sing, that they shall hear I am not afraid.
[Sings.]

The ousel cock, so black of hue,
  With orange-tawny bill,
The throstle with his note so true,
  The wren with little quill.

TITANIA.
[Waking.] What angel wakes me from my flowery bed?
BOTTOM.
[Sings.]

The finch, the sparrow, and the lark,
  The plain-song cuckoo gray,
Whose note full many a man doth mark,
  And dares not answer nay.

for, indeed, who would set his wit to so foolish a bird? Who would give a bird the lie, though he cry 'cuckoo' never so?
TITANIA.
I pray thee, gentle mortal, sing again.
Mine ear is much enamour'd of thy note.
So is mine eye enthrallèd to thy shape;

And thy fair virtue's force perforce doth move me,
On the first view, to say, to swear, I love thee.
BOTTOM.
Methinks, mistress, you should have little reason for that. And yet, to say the truth, reason and love keep little company together nowadays. The more the pity that some honest neighbours will not make them friends. Nay, I can gleek upon occasion.
TITANIA.
Thou art as wise as thou art beautiful.
BOTTOM.
Not so, neither; but if I had wit enough to get out of this wood, I have enough to serve mine own turn.
TITANIA.
Out of this wood do not desire to go.
Thou shalt remain here whether thou wilt or no.
I am a spirit of no common rate.
The summer still doth tend upon my state;
And I do love thee: therefore, go with me.
I'll give thee fairies to attend on thee;
And they shall fetch thee jewels from the deep,
And sing, while thou on pressèd flowers dost sleep.
And I will purge thy mortal grossness so
That thou shalt like an airy spirit go.—
Peaseblossom! Cobweb! Moth! and Mustardseed!
Enter four Fairies.
PEASEBLOSSOM.
Ready.
COBWEB.
And I.
MOTH.
And I.
MUSTARDSEED.
And I.
ALL.
Where shall we go?

TITANIA.
Be kind and courteous to this gentleman;
Hop in his walks and gambol in his eyes;
Feed him with apricocks and dewberries,
With purple grapes, green figs, and mulberries;
The honey-bags steal from the humble-bees,
And for night-tapers, crop their waxen thighs,
And light them at the fiery glow-worm's eyes,
To have my love to bed and to arise;
And pluck the wings from painted butterflies,
To fan the moonbeams from his sleeping eyes.
Nod to him, elves, and do him courtesies.
PEASEBLOSSOM.
Hail, mortal!
COBWEB.
Hail!
MOTH.
Hail!
MUSTARDSEED.
Hail!
BOTTOM.
I cry your worships mercy, heartily.—I beseech your worship's name.
COBWEB.
Cobweb.
BOTTOM.
I shall desire you of more acquaintance, good Master Cobweb. If I cut my finger, I shall make bold with you.—Your name, honest gentleman?
PEASEBLOSSOM.
Peaseblossom.
BOTTOM.
I pray you, commend me to Mistress Squash, your mother, and to Master Peascod, your father. Good Master Peaseblossom, I shall desire you of more acquaintance too.—Your name, I beseech you, sir?
MUSTARDSEED.
Mustardseed.

BOTTOM.

Good Master Mustardseed, I know your patience well. That same cowardly giant-like ox-beef hath devoured many a gentleman of your house. I promise you, your kindred hath made my eyes water ere now. I desire you of more acquaintance, good Master Mustardseed.

TITANIA.

Come, wait upon him; lead him to my bower.
  The moon, methinks, looks with a watery eye,
And when she weeps, weeps every little flower,
  Lamenting some enforced chastity.
Tie up my love's tongue, bring him silently.

[Exeunt.]

SCENE II.
Another part of the wood

Enter Oberon.
OBERON.
I wonder if Titania be awak'd;
Then, what it was that next came in her eye,
Which she must dote on in extremity.
Enter Puck.
Here comes my messenger. How now, mad spirit?
What night-rule now about this haunted grove?
PUCK.
My mistress with a monster is in love.
Near to her close and consecrated bower,
While she was in her dull and sleeping hour,
A crew of patches, rude mechanicals,
That work for bread upon Athenian stalls,
Were met together to rehearse a play
Intended for great Theseus' nuptial day.
The shallowest thick-skin of that barren sort
Who Pyramus presented in their sport,
Forsook his scene and enter'd in a brake.
When I did him at this advantage take,
An ass's nole I fixed on his head.
Anon, his Thisbe must be answerèd,
And forth my mimic comes. When they him spy,
As wild geese that the creeping fowler eye,
Or russet-pated choughs, many in sort,
Rising and cawing at the gun's report,
Sever themselves and madly sweep the sky,
So at his sight away his fellows fly,
And at our stamp, here o'er and o'er one falls;
He murder cries, and help from Athens calls.
Their sense thus weak, lost with their fears, thus strong,

Made senseless things begin to do them wrong;
For briers and thorns at their apparel snatch;
Some sleeves, some hats, from yielders all things catch.
I led them on in this distracted fear,
And left sweet Pyramus translated there.
When in that moment, so it came to pass,
Titania wak'd, and straightway lov'd an ass.
OBERON.
This falls out better than I could devise.
But hast thou yet latch'd the Athenian's eyes
With the love-juice, as I did bid thee do?
PUCK.
I took him sleeping—that is finish'd too—
And the Athenian woman by his side,
That, when he wak'd, of force she must be ey'd.
Enter Demetrius and Hermia.
OBERON.
Stand close. This is the same Athenian.
PUCK.
This is the woman, but not this the man.
DEMETRIUS.
O why rebuke you him that loves you so?
Lay breath so bitter on your bitter foe.
HERMIA.
Now I but chide, but I should use thee worse,
For thou, I fear, hast given me cause to curse.
If thou hast slain Lysander in his sleep,
Being o'er shoes in blood, plunge in the deep,
And kill me too.
The sun was not so true unto the day
As he to me. Would he have stol'n away
From sleeping Hermia? I'll believe as soon
This whole earth may be bor'd, and that the moon
May through the centre creep and so displease
Her brother's noontide with th' Antipodes.

It cannot be but thou hast murder'd him.
So should a murderer look, so dead, so grim.
DEMETRIUS.
So should the murder'd look, and so should I,
Pierc'd through the heart with your stern cruelty.
Yet you, the murderer, look as bright, as clear,
As yonder Venus in her glimmering sphere.
HERMIA.
What's this to my Lysander? Where is he?
Ah, good Demetrius, wilt thou give him me?
DEMETRIUS.
I had rather give his carcass to my hounds.
HERMIA.
Out, dog! Out, cur! Thou driv'st me past the bounds
Of maiden's patience. Hast thou slain him, then?
Henceforth be never number'd among men!
O once tell true; tell true, even for my sake!
Durst thou have look'd upon him, being awake,
And hast thou kill'd him sleeping? O brave touch!
Could not a worm, an adder, do so much?
An adder did it; for with doubler tongue
Than thine, thou serpent, never adder stung.
DEMETRIUS.
You spend your passion on a mispris'd mood:
I am not guilty of Lysander's blood;
Nor is he dead, for aught that I can tell.
HERMIA.
I pray thee, tell me then that he is well.
DEMETRIUS.
And if I could, what should I get therefore?
HERMIA.
A privilege never to see me more.
And from thy hated presence part I so:
See me no more, whether he be dead or no.
[Exit.]

DEMETRIUS.
There is no following her in this fierce vein.
Here, therefore, for a while I will remain.
So sorrow's heaviness doth heavier grow
For debt that bankrupt sleep doth sorrow owe;
Which now in some slight measure it will pay,
If for his tender here I make some stay.
[Lies down.]
OBERON.
What hast thou done? Thou hast mistaken quite,
And laid the love-juice on some true-love's sight.
Of thy misprision must perforce ensue
Some true love turn'd, and not a false turn'd true.
PUCK.
Then fate o'er-rules, that, one man holding troth,
A million fail, confounding oath on oath.
OBERON.
About the wood go swifter than the wind,
And Helena of Athens look thou find.
All fancy-sick she is, and pale of cheer
With sighs of love, that costs the fresh blood dear.
By some illusion see thou bring her here;
I'll charm his eyes against she do appear.
PUCK.
I go, I go; look how I go,
Swifter than arrow from the Tartar's bow.
[Exit.]
OBERON.
Flower of this purple dye,
Hit with Cupid's archery,
Sink in apple of his eye.
When his love he doth espy,
Let her shine as gloriously
As the Venus of the sky.—

When thou wak'st, if she be by,
Beg of her for remedy.

Enter Puck.

PUCK.
Captain of our fairy band,
Helena is here at hand,
And the youth mistook by me,
Pleading for a lover's fee.
Shall we their fond pageant see?
Lord, what fools these mortals be!

OBERON.
Stand aside. The noise they make
Will cause Demetrius to awake.

PUCK.
Then will two at once woo one.
That must needs be sport alone;
And those things do best please me
That befall prepost'rously.

Enter Lysander and Helena.

LYSANDER.
Why should you think that I should woo in scorn?
Scorn and derision never come in tears.
Look when I vow, I weep; and vows so born,
In their nativity all truth appears.
How can these things in me seem scorn to you,
Bearing the badge of faith, to prove them true?

HELENA.
You do advance your cunning more and more.
When truth kills truth, O devilish-holy fray!
These vows are Hermia's: will you give her o'er?
Weigh oath with oath, and you will nothing weigh:
Your vows to her and me, put in two scales,
Will even weigh; and both as light as tales.

LYSANDER.
I had no judgment when to her I swore.

HELENA.
Nor none, in my mind, now you give her o'er.
LYSANDER.
Demetrius loves her, and he loves not you.
DEMETRIUS.
[Waking.] O Helen, goddess, nymph, perfect, divine!
To what, my love, shall I compare thine eyne?
Crystal is muddy. O how ripe in show
Thy lips, those kissing cherries, tempting grow!
That pure congealèd white, high Taurus' snow,
Fann'd with the eastern wind, turns to a crow
When thou hold'st up thy hand. O, let me kiss
This princess of pure white, this seal of bliss!
HELENA.
O spite! O hell! I see you all are bent
To set against me for your merriment.
If you were civil, and knew courtesy,
You would not do me thus much injury.
Can you not hate me, as I know you do,
But you must join in souls to mock me too?
If you were men, as men you are in show,
You would not use a gentle lady so;
To vow, and swear, and superpraise my parts,
When I am sure you hate me with your hearts.
You both are rivals, and love Hermia;
And now both rivals, to mock Helena.
A trim exploit, a manly enterprise,
To conjure tears up in a poor maid's eyes
With your derision! None of noble sort
Would so offend a virgin, and extort
A poor soul's patience, all to make you sport.
LYSANDER.
You are unkind, Demetrius; be not so,
For you love Hermia; this you know I know.
And here, with all good will, with all my heart,

In Hermia's love I yield you up my part;
And yours of Helena to me bequeath,
Whom I do love and will do till my death.
HELENA.
Never did mockers waste more idle breath.
DEMETRIUS.
Lysander, keep thy Hermia; I will none.
If e'er I lov'd her, all that love is gone.
My heart to her but as guest-wise sojourn'd;
And now to Helen is it home return'd,
There to remain.
LYSANDER.
Helen, it is not so.
DEMETRIUS.
Disparage not the faith thou dost not know,
Lest to thy peril thou aby it dear.
Look where thy love comes; yonder is thy dear.
Enter Hermia.
HERMIA.
Dark night, that from the eye his function takes,
The ear more quick of apprehension makes;
Wherein it doth impair the seeing sense,
It pays the hearing double recompense.
Thou art not by mine eye, Lysander, found;
Mine ear, I thank it, brought me to thy sound.
But why unkindly didst thou leave me so?
LYSANDER.
Why should he stay whom love doth press to go?
HERMIA.
What love could press Lysander from my side?
LYSANDER.
Lysander's love, that would not let him bide,
Fair Helena, who more engilds the night
Than all yon fiery oes and eyes of light.

Why seek'st thou me? Could not this make thee know
The hate I bare thee made me leave thee so?
HERMIA.
You speak not as you think; it cannot be.
HELENA.
Lo, she is one of this confederacy!
Now I perceive they have conjoin'd all three
To fashion this false sport in spite of me.
Injurious Hermia, most ungrateful maid!
Have you conspir'd, have you with these contriv'd,
To bait me with this foul derision?
Is all the counsel that we two have shar'd,
The sisters' vows, the hours that we have spent,
When we have chid the hasty-footed time
For parting us—O, is all forgot?
All school-days' friendship, childhood innocence?
We, Hermia, like two artificial gods,
Have with our needles created both one flower,
Both on one sampler, sitting on one cushion,
Both warbling of one song, both in one key,
As if our hands, our sides, voices, and minds,
Had been incorporate. So we grew together,
Like to a double cherry, seeming parted,
But yet a union in partition,
Two lovely berries moulded on one stem;
So, with two seeming bodies, but one heart;
Two of the first, like coats in heraldry,
Due but to one, and crownèd with one crest.
And will you rent our ancient love asunder,
To join with men in scorning your poor friend?
It is not friendly, 'tis not maidenly.
Our sex, as well as I, may chide you for it,
Though I alone do feel the injury.

HERMIA.
I am amazèd at your passionate words:
I scorn you not; it seems that you scorn me.
HELENA.
Have you not set Lysander, as in scorn,
To follow me, and praise my eyes and face?
And made your other love, Demetrius,
Who even but now did spurn me with his foot,
To call me goddess, nymph, divine and rare,
Precious, celestial? Wherefore speaks he this
To her he hates? And wherefore doth Lysander
Deny your love, so rich within his soul,
And tender me, forsooth, affection,
But by your setting on, by your consent?
What though I be not so in grace as you,
So hung upon with love, so fortunate,
But miserable most, to love unlov'd?
This you should pity rather than despise.
HERMIA.
I understand not what you mean by this.
HELENA.
Ay, do. Persever, counterfeit sad looks,
Make mouths upon me when I turn my back,
Wink each at other; hold the sweet jest up.
This sport, well carried, shall be chronicled.
If you have any pity, grace, or manners,
You would not make me such an argument.
But fare ye well. 'Tis partly my own fault,
Which death, or absence, soon shall remedy.
LYSANDER.
Stay, gentle Helena; hear my excuse;
My love, my life, my soul, fair Helena!
HELENA.
O excellent!

HERMIA.
Sweet, do not scorn her so.
DEMETRIUS.
If she cannot entreat, I can compel.
LYSANDER.
Thou canst compel no more than she entreat;
Thy threats have no more strength than her weak prayers.
Helen, I love thee, by my life I do;
I swear by that which I will lose for thee
To prove him false that says I love thee not.
DEMETRIUS.
I say I love thee more than he can do.
LYSANDER.
If thou say so, withdraw, and prove it too.
DEMETRIUS.
Quick, come.
HERMIA.
Lysander, whereto tends all this?
LYSANDER.
Away, you Ethiope!
DEMETRIUS.
No, no. He will
Seem to break loose. Take on as you would follow,
But yet come not. You are a tame man, go!
LYSANDER.
Hang off, thou cat, thou burr! Vile thing, let loose,
Or I will shake thee from me like a serpent.
HERMIA.
Why are you grown so rude? What change is this,
Sweet love?
LYSANDER.
Thy love? Out, tawny Tartar, out!
Out, loathèd medicine! O hated potion, hence!
HERMIA.
Do you not jest?

HELENA.
Yes, sooth, and so do you.
LYSANDER.
Demetrius, I will keep my word with thee.
DEMETRIUS.
I would I had your bond; for I perceive
A weak bond holds you; I'll not trust your word.
LYSANDER.
What, should I hurt her, strike her, kill her dead?
Although I hate her, I'll not harm her so.
HERMIA.
What, can you do me greater harm than hate?
Hate me? Wherefore? O me! what news, my love?
Am not I Hermia? Are not you Lysander?
I am as fair now as I was erewhile.
Since night you lov'd me; yet since night you left me.
Why then, you left me—O, the gods forbid!—
In earnest, shall I say?
LYSANDER.
Ay, by my life;
And never did desire to see thee more.
Therefore be out of hope, of question, of doubt;
Be certain, nothing truer; 'tis no jest
That I do hate thee and love Helena.
HERMIA.
O me! You juggler! You cankerblossom!
You thief of love! What! have you come by night
And stol'n my love's heart from him?
HELENA.
Fine, i' faith!
Have you no modesty, no maiden shame,
No touch of bashfulness? What, will you tear
Impatient answers from my gentle tongue?
Fie, fie, you counterfeit, you puppet, you!

HERMIA.
Puppet! Why so? Ay, that way goes the game.
Now I perceive that she hath made compare
Between our statures; she hath urg'd her height;
And with her personage, her tall personage,
Her height, forsooth, she hath prevail'd with him.
And are you grown so high in his esteem
Because I am so dwarfish and so low?
How low am I, thou painted maypole? Speak,
How low am I? I am not yet so low
But that my nails can reach unto thine eyes.
HELENA.
I pray you, though you mock me, gentlemen,
Let her not hurt me. I was never curst;
I have no gift at all in shrewishness;
I am a right maid for my cowardice;
Let her not strike me. You perhaps may think,
Because she is something lower than myself,
That I can match her.
HERMIA.
Lower! Hark, again.
HELENA.
Good Hermia, do not be so bitter with me.
I evermore did love you, Hermia,
Did ever keep your counsels, never wrong'd you,
Save that, in love unto Demetrius,
I told him of your stealth unto this wood.
He follow'd you; for love I follow'd him;
But he hath chid me hence, and threaten'd me
To strike me, spurn me, nay, to kill me too:
And now, so you will let me quiet go,
To Athens will I bear my folly back,
And follow you no further. Let me go:
You see how simple and how fond I am.

HERMIA.
Why, get you gone. Who is't that hinders you?
HELENA.
A foolish heart that I leave here behind.
HERMIA.
What! with Lysander?
HELENA.
With Demetrius.
LYSANDER.
Be not afraid; she shall not harm thee, Helena.
DEMETRIUS.
No, sir, she shall not, though you take her part.
HELENA.
O, when she's angry, she is keen and shrewd.
She was a vixen when she went to school,
And though she be but little, she is fierce.
HERMIA.
Little again! Nothing but low and little?
Why will you suffer her to flout me thus?
Let me come to her.
LYSANDER.
Get you gone, you dwarf;
You minimus, of hind'ring knot-grass made;
You bead, you acorn.
DEMETRIUS.
You are too officious
In her behalf that scorns your services.
Let her alone. Speak not of Helena;
Take not her part; for if thou dost intend
Never so little show of love to her,
Thou shalt aby it.
LYSANDER.
Now she holds me not.
Now follow, if thou dar'st, to try whose right,
Of thine or mine, is most in Helena.

DEMETRIUS.
Follow! Nay, I'll go with thee, cheek by jole.
[Exeunt Lysander and Demetrius.]
HERMIA.
You, mistress, all this coil is long of you.
Nay, go not back.
HELENA.
I will not trust you, I,
Nor longer stay in your curst company.
Your hands than mine are quicker for a fray.
My legs are longer though, to run away.
[Exit.]
HERMIA.
I am amaz'd, and know not what to say.
[Exit, pursuing Helena.]
OBERON.
This is thy negligence: still thou mistak'st,
Or else commit'st thy knaveries willfully.
PUCK.
Believe me, king of shadows, I mistook.
Did not you tell me I should know the man
By the Athenian garments he had on?
And so far blameless proves my enterprise
That I have 'nointed an Athenian's eyes:
And so far am I glad it so did sort,
As this their jangling I esteem a sport.
OBERON.
Thou seest these lovers seek a place to fight.
Hie therefore, Robin, overcast the night;
The starry welkin cover thou anon
With drooping fog, as black as Acheron,
And lead these testy rivals so astray
As one come not within another's way.
Like to Lysander sometime frame thy tongue,
Then stir Demetrius up with bitter wrong;

And sometime rail thou like Demetrius.
And from each other look thou lead them thus,
Till o'er their brows death-counterfeiting sleep
With leaden legs and batty wings doth creep.
Then crush this herb into Lysander's eye,
Whose liquor hath this virtuous property,
To take from thence all error with his might
And make his eyeballs roll with wonted sight.
When they next wake, all this derision
Shall seem a dream and fruitless vision;
And back to Athens shall the lovers wend,
With league whose date till death shall never end.
Whiles I in this affair do thee employ,
I'll to my queen, and beg her Indian boy;
And then I will her charmèd eye release
From monster's view, and all things shall be peace.
PUCK.
My fairy lord, this must be done with haste,
For night's swift dragons cut the clouds full fast;
And yonder shines Aurora's harbinger,
At whose approach, ghosts wandering here and there
Troop home to churchyards. Damnèd spirits all,
That in cross-ways and floods have burial,
Already to their wormy beds are gone;
For fear lest day should look their shames upon,
They wilfully themselves exile from light,
And must for aye consort with black-brow'd night.
OBERON.
But we are spirits of another sort:
I with the morning's love have oft made sport;
And, like a forester, the groves may tread
Even till the eastern gate, all fiery-red,
Opening on Neptune with fair blessèd beams,
Turns into yellow gold his salt-green streams.

But, notwithstanding, haste, make no delay.
We may effect this business yet ere day.

[Exit Oberon.]

PUCK.
Up and down, up and down,
I will lead them up and down.
I am fear'd in field and town.
Goblin, lead them up and down.
Here comes one.

Enter Lysander.

LYSANDER.
Where art thou, proud Demetrius? Speak thou now.

PUCK.
Here, villain, drawn and ready. Where art thou?

LYSANDER.
I will be with thee straight.

PUCK.
Follow me then to plainer ground.

[Exit Lysander as following the voice.]

Enter Demetrius.

DEMETRIUS.
Lysander, speak again.
Thou runaway, thou coward, art thou fled?
Speak. In some bush? Where dost thou hide thy head?

PUCK.
Thou coward, art thou bragging to the stars,
Telling the bushes that thou look'st for wars,
And wilt not come? Come, recreant, come, thou child!
I'll whip thee with a rod. He is defil'd
That draws a sword on thee.

DEMETRIUS.
Yea, art thou there?

PUCK.
Follow my voice; we'll try no manhood here.

[Exeunt.]

Enter Lysander.

LYSANDER.
He goes before me, and still dares me on;
When I come where he calls, then he is gone.
The villain is much lighter-heel'd than I:
I follow'd fast, but faster he did fly,
That fallen am I in dark uneven way,
And here will rest me. Come, thou gentle day!
[Lies down.] For if but once thou show me thy grey light,
I'll find Demetrius, and revenge this spite.

[Sleeps.]

Enter Puck and Demetrius.

PUCK.
Ho, ho, ho! Coward, why com'st thou not?

DEMETRIUS.
Abide me, if thou dar'st; for well I wot
Thou runn'st before me, shifting every place,
And dar'st not stand, nor look me in the face.
Where art thou?

PUCK.
Come hither; I am here.

DEMETRIUS.
Nay, then, thou mock'st me. Thou shalt buy this dear
If ever I thy face by daylight see:
Now go thy way. Faintness constraineth me
To measure out my length on this cold bed.
By day's approach look to be visited.

[Lies down and sleeps.]

Enter Helena.

HELENA.
O weary night, O long and tedious night,
   Abate thy hours! Shine, comforts, from the east,
That I may back to Athens by daylight,
   From these that my poor company detest.
And sleep, that sometimes shuts up sorrow's eye,
Steal me awhile from mine own company.

[Sleeps.]

PUCK.
   Yet but three? Come one more.

Two of both kinds makes up four.
Here she comes, curst and sad.
Cupid is a knavish lad
Thus to make poor females mad.

Enter Hermia.

HERMIA.
Never so weary, never so in woe,
Bedabbled with the dew, and torn with briers,
I can no further crawl, no further go;
My legs can keep no pace with my desires.
Here will I rest me till the break of day.
Heavens shield Lysander, if they mean a fray!

[Lies down.]

PUCK.
On the ground
Sleep sound.
I'll apply
To your eye,
Gentle lover, remedy.

[Squeezing the juice on Lysander's eye.]

When thou wak'st,
Thou tak'st
True delight
In the sight
Of thy former lady's eye.
And the country proverb known,
That every man should take his own,
In your waking shall be shown:
Jack shall have Jill;
Nought shall go ill;
The man shall have his mare again, and all shall be well.

[Exit Puck.]

ACT IV

SCENE I.
The Wood

Lysander, Demetrius, Helena and Hermia still asleep.
Enter Titania and Bottom; Peaseblossom, Cobweb, Moth,
Mustardseed and other Fairies attending; Oberon behind, unseen.

TITANIA.
Come, sit thee down upon this flowery bed,
  While I thy amiable cheeks do coy,
And stick musk-roses in thy sleek smooth head,
  And kiss thy fair large ears, my gentle joy.

BOTTOM.
Where's Peaseblossom?

PEASEBLOSSOM.
Ready.

BOTTOM.
Scratch my head, Peaseblossom. Where's Monsieur Cobweb?

COBWEB.
Ready.

BOTTOM.
Monsieur Cobweb; good monsieur, get you your weapons in your hand and kill me a red-hipped humble-bee on the top of a thistle; and, good monsieur, bring me the honey-bag. Do not fret yourself too much in the action, monsieur; and, good monsieur, have a care the honey-bag break not; I would be loath to have you overflown with a honey-bag, signior. Where's Monsieur Mustardseed?

MUSTARDSEED.
Ready.

BOTTOM.
Give me your neaf, Monsieur Mustardseed. Pray you, leave your courtesy, good monsieur.
MUSTARDSEED.
What's your will?
BOTTOM.
Nothing, good monsieur, but to help Cavalery Cobweb to scratch. I must to the barber's, monsieur, for methinks I am marvellous hairy about the face; and I am such a tender ass, if my hair do but tickle me, I must scratch.
TITANIA.
What, wilt thou hear some music, my sweet love?
BOTTOM.
I have a reasonable good ear in music. Let us have the tongs and the bones.
TITANIA.
Or say, sweet love, what thou desirest to eat.
BOTTOM.
Truly, a peck of provender; I could munch your good dry oats. Methinks I have a great desire to a bottle of hay: good hay, sweet hay, hath no fellow.
TITANIA.
I have a venturous fairy that shall seek
The squirrel's hoard, and fetch thee new nuts.
BOTTOM.
I had rather have a handful or two of dried peas. But, I pray you, let none of your people stir me; I have an exposition of sleep come upon me.
TITANIA.
Sleep thou, and I will wind thee in my arms.
Fairies, be gone, and be all ways away.
So doth the woodbine the sweet honeysuckle
Gently entwist, the female ivy so
Enrings the barky fingers of the elm.
O, how I love thee! How I dote on thee!
[They sleep.]
Oberon advances. Enter Puck.
OBERON.
Welcome, good Robin. Seest thou this sweet sight?

Her dotage now I do begin to pity.
For, meeting her of late behind the wood,
Seeking sweet favours for this hateful fool,
I did upbraid her and fall out with her:
For she his hairy temples then had rounded
With coronet of fresh and fragrant flowers;
And that same dew, which sometime on the buds
Was wont to swell like round and orient pearls,
Stood now within the pretty flouriets' eyes,
Like tears that did their own disgrace bewail.
When I had at my pleasure taunted her,
And she in mild terms begg'd my patience,
I then did ask of her her changeling child;
Which straight she gave me, and her fairy sent
To bear him to my bower in fairyland.
And now I have the boy, I will undo
This hateful imperfection of her eyes.
And, gentle Puck, take this transformèd scalp
From off the head of this Athenian swain,
That he awaking when the other do,
May all to Athens back again repair,
And think no more of this night's accidents
But as the fierce vexation of a dream.
But first I will release the Fairy Queen.
[Touching her eyes with an herb.]
   Be as thou wast wont to be;
   See as thou was wont to see.
   Dian's bud o'er Cupid's flower
   Hath such force and blessed power.
Now, my Titania, wake you, my sweet queen.
TITANIA.
My Oberon, what visions have I seen!
Methought I was enamour'd of an ass.
OBERON.
There lies your love.

TITANIA.
How came these things to pass?
O, how mine eyes do loathe his visage now!
OBERON.
Silence awhile.—Robin, take off this head.
Titania, music call; and strike more dead
Than common sleep, of all these five the sense.
TITANIA.
Music, ho, music, such as charmeth sleep.
PUCK.
Now when thou wak'st, with thine own fool's eyes peep.
OBERON.
Sound, music.
[Still music.]
Come, my queen, take hands with me,
And rock the ground whereon these sleepers be.
Now thou and I are new in amity,
And will tomorrow midnight solemnly
Dance in Duke Theseus' house triumphantly,
And bless it to all fair prosperity:
There shall the pairs of faithful lovers be
Wedded, with Theseus, all in jollity.
PUCK.
Fairy king, attend and mark.
I do hear the morning lark.
OBERON.
Then, my queen, in silence sad,
Trip we after night's shade.
We the globe can compass soon,
Swifter than the wand'ring moon.
TITANIA.
Come, my lord, and in our flight,
Tell me how it came this night
That I sleeping here was found
With these mortals on the ground.

[Exeunt. Horns sound within.]
Enter Theseus, Hippolyta, Egeus and Train.
THESEUS.
Go, one of you, find out the forester;
For now our observation is perform'd;
And since we have the vaward of the day,
My love shall hear the music of my hounds.
Uncouple in the western valley; let them go.
Dispatch I say, and find the forester.
[Exit an Attendant.]
We will, fair queen, up to the mountain's top,
And mark the musical confusion
Of hounds and echo in conjunction.
HIPPOLYTA.
I was with Hercules and Cadmus once,
When in a wood of Crete they bay'd the bear
With hounds of Sparta. Never did I hear
Such gallant chiding; for, besides the groves,
The skies, the fountains, every region near
Seem'd all one mutual cry. I never heard
So musical a discord, such sweet thunder.
THESEUS.
My hounds are bred out of the Spartan kind,
So flew'd, so sanded; and their heads are hung
With ears that sweep away the morning dew;
Crook-knee'd and dewlap'd like Thessalian bulls;
Slow in pursuit, but match'd in mouth like bells,
Each under each. A cry more tuneable
Was never holla'd to, nor cheer'd with horn,
In Crete, in Sparta, nor in Thessaly.
Judge when you hear.—But, soft, what nymphs are these?
EGEUS.
My lord, this is my daughter here asleep,
And this Lysander; this Demetrius is;

This Helena, old Nedar's Helena:
I wonder of their being here together.
THESEUS.
No doubt they rose up early to observe
The rite of May; and, hearing our intent,
Came here in grace of our solemnity.
But speak, Egeus; is not this the day
That Hermia should give answer of her choice?
EGEUS.
It is, my lord.
THESEUS.
Go, bid the huntsmen wake them with their horns.
Horns, and shout within. Demetrius, Lysander, Hermia and Helena wake and start up.
Good morrow, friends. Saint Valentine is past.
Begin these wood-birds but to couple now?
LYSANDER.
Pardon, my lord.
He and the rest kneel to Theseus.
THESEUS.
I pray you all, stand up.
I know you two are rival enemies.
How comes this gentle concord in the world,
That hatred is so far from jealousy
To sleep by hate, and fear no enmity?
LYSANDER.
My lord, I shall reply amazedly,
Half sleep, half waking; but as yet, I swear,
I cannot truly say how I came here.
But, as I think (for truly would I speak)
And now I do bethink me, so it is:
I came with Hermia hither. Our intent
Was to be gone from Athens, where we might be
Without the peril of the Athenian law.

EGEUS.
Enough, enough, my lord; you have enough.
I beg the law, the law upon his head.
They would have stol'n away, they would, Demetrius,
Thereby to have defeated you and me:
You of your wife, and me of my consent,
Of my consent that she should be your wife.
DEMETRIUS.
My lord, fair Helen told me of their stealth,
Of this their purpose hither to this wood;
And I in fury hither follow'd them,
Fair Helena in fancy following me.
But, my good lord, I wot not by what power,
(But by some power it is) my love to Hermia,
Melted as the snow, seems to me now
As the remembrance of an idle gaud
Which in my childhood I did dote upon;
And all the faith, the virtue of my heart,
The object and the pleasure of mine eye,
Is only Helena. To her, my lord,
Was I betroth'd ere I saw Hermia.
But like a sickness did I loathe this food.
But, as in health, come to my natural taste,
Now I do wish it, love it, long for it,
And will for evermore be true to it.
THESEUS.
Fair lovers, you are fortunately met.
Of this discourse we more will hear anon.
Egeus, I will overbear your will;
For in the temple, by and by with us,
These couples shall eternally be knit.
And, for the morning now is something worn,
Our purpos'd hunting shall be set aside.
Away with us to Athens. Three and three,

We'll hold a feast in great solemnity.
Come, Hippolyta.
[Exeunt Theseus, Hippolyta, Egeus and Train.]
DEMETRIUS.
These things seem small and undistinguishable,
Like far-off mountains turnèd into clouds.
HERMIA.
Methinks I see these things with parted eye,
When everything seems double.
HELENA.
So methinks.
And I have found Demetrius like a jewel,
Mine own, and not mine own.
DEMETRIUS.
Are you sure
That we are awake? It seems to me
That yet we sleep, we dream. Do not you think
The Duke was here, and bid us follow him?
HERMIA.
Yea, and my father.
HELENA.
And Hippolyta.
LYSANDER.
And he did bid us follow to the temple.
DEMETRIUS.
Why, then, we are awake: let's follow him,
And by the way let us recount our dreams.
[Exeunt.]
BOTTOM.
[Waking.] When my cue comes, call me, and I will answer. My next is 'Most fair Pyramus.' Heigh-ho! Peter Quince! Flute, the bellows-mender! Snout, the tinker! Starveling! God's my life! Stol'n hence, and left me asleep! I have had a most rare vision. I have had a dream, past the wit of man to say what dream it was. Man is but an ass if he go about to expound this dream. Methought I was—there is no man can tell what. Methought I

was, and methought I had—but man is but a patched fool if he will offer to say what methought I had. The eye of man hath not heard, the ear of man hath not seen, man's hand is not able to taste, his tongue to conceive, nor his heart to report, what my dream was. I will get Peter Quince to write a ballad of this dream: it shall be called 'Bottom's Dream', because it hath no bottom; and I will sing it in the latter end of a play, before the Duke. Peradventure, to make it the more gracious, I shall sing it at her death.
[Exit.]

SCENE II.
Athens. A Room in Quince's House

Enter Quince, Flute, Snout and Starveling.
QUINCE.
Have you sent to Bottom's house? Is he come home yet?
STARVELING.
He cannot be heard of. Out of doubt he is transported.
FLUTE.
If he come not, then the play is marred. It goes not forward, doth it?
QUINCE.
It is not possible. You have not a man in all Athens able to discharge Pyramus but he.
FLUTE.
No, he hath simply the best wit of any handicraft man in Athens.
QUINCE.
Yea, and the best person too, and he is a very paramour for a sweet voice.
FLUTE.
You must say paragon. A paramour is, God bless us, a thing of naught.
Enter Snug.
SNUG
Masters, the Duke is coming from the temple, and there is two or three lords and ladies more married. If our sport had gone forward, we had all been made men.
FLUTE.
O sweet bully Bottom! Thus hath he lost sixpence a day during his life; he could not have 'scaped sixpence a day. An the Duke had not given him sixpence a day for playing Pyramus, I'll be hanged. He would have deserved it: sixpence a day in Pyramus, or nothing.
Enter Bottom.
BOTTOM.
Where are these lads? Where are these hearts?
QUINCE.
Bottom! O most courageous day! O most happy hour!

BOTTOM.
Masters, I am to discourse wonders: but ask me not what; for if I tell you, I am not true Athenian. I will tell you everything, right as it fell out.
QUINCE.
Let us hear, sweet Bottom.
BOTTOM.
Not a word of me. All that I will tell you is, that the Duke hath dined. Get your apparel together, good strings to your beards, new ribbons to your pumps; meet presently at the palace; every man look o'er his part. For the short and the long is, our play is preferred. In any case, let Thisbe have clean linen; and let not him that plays the lion pare his nails, for they shall hang out for the lion's claws. And most dear actors, eat no onions nor garlick, for we are to utter sweet breath; and I do not doubt but to hear them say it is a sweet comedy. No more words. Away! Go, away!
[Exeunt.]

ACT V

SCENE I.
Athens. An Apartment in the Palace of Theseus

Enter Theseus, Hippolyta, Philostrate, Lords and Attendants.
HIPPOLYTA.
'Tis strange, my Theseus, that these lovers speak of.
THESEUS.
More strange than true. I never may believe
These antique fables, nor these fairy toys.
Lovers and madmen have such seething brains,
Such shaping fantasies, that apprehend
More than cool reason ever comprehends.
The lunatic, the lover, and the poet
Are of imagination all compact:
One sees more devils than vast hell can hold;
That is the madman: the lover, all as frantic,
Sees Helen's beauty in a brow of Egypt:
The poet's eye, in a fine frenzy rolling,
Doth glance from heaven to earth, from earth to heaven;
And as imagination bodies forth
The forms of things unknown, the poet's pen
Turns them to shapes, and gives to airy nothing
A local habitation and a name.
Such tricks hath strong imagination,
That if it would but apprehend some joy,
It comprehends some bringer of that joy.
Or in the night, imagining some fear,
How easy is a bush supposed a bear?
HIPPOLYTA.
But all the story of the night told over,

And all their minds transfigur'd so together,
More witnesseth than fancy's images,
And grows to something of great constancy;
But, howsoever, strange and admirable.
Enter lovers: Lysander, Demetrius, Hermia and Helena.
THESEUS.
Here come the lovers, full of joy and mirth.
Joy, gentle friends, joy and fresh days of love
Accompany your hearts!
LYSANDER.
More than to us
Wait in your royal walks, your board, your bed!
THESEUS.
Come now; what masques, what dances shall we have,
To wear away this long age of three hours
Between our after-supper and bed-time?
Where is our usual manager of mirth?
What revels are in hand? Is there no play
To ease the anguish of a torturing hour?
Call Philostrate.
PHILOSTRATE.
Here, mighty Theseus.
THESEUS.
Say, what abridgment have you for this evening?
What masque? What music? How shall we beguile
The lazy time, if not with some delight?
PHILOSTRATE.
There is a brief how many sports are ripe.
Make choice of which your Highness will see first.
[Giving a paper.]
THESEUS.
[Reads] 'The battle with the Centaurs, to be sung
By an Athenian eunuch to the harp.'
We'll none of that. That have I told my love
In glory of my kinsman Hercules.

'The riot of the tipsy Bacchanals,
Tearing the Thracian singer in their rage?'
That is an old device, and it was play'd
When I from Thebes came last a conqueror.
'The thrice three Muses mourning for the death
Of learning, late deceas'd in beggary.'
That is some satire, keen and critical,
Not sorting with a nuptial ceremony.
'A tedious brief scene of young Pyramus
And his love Thisbe; very tragical mirth.'
Merry and tragical? Tedious and brief?
That is hot ice and wondrous strange snow.
How shall we find the concord of this discord?
PHILOSTRATE.
A play there is, my lord, some ten words long,
Which is as brief as I have known a play;
But by ten words, my lord, it is too long,
Which makes it tedious. For in all the play
There is not one word apt, one player fitted.
And tragical, my noble lord, it is.
For Pyramus therein doth kill himself,
Which, when I saw rehears'd, I must confess,
Made mine eyes water; but more merry tears
The passion of loud laughter never shed.
THESEUS.
What are they that do play it?
PHILOSTRATE.
Hard-handed men that work in Athens here,
Which never labour'd in their minds till now;
And now have toil'd their unbreath'd memories
With this same play against your nuptial.
THESEUS.
And we will hear it.
PHILOSTRATE.
No, my noble lord,

It is not for you: I have heard it over,
And it is nothing, nothing in the world;
Unless you can find sport in their intents,
Extremely stretch'd and conn'd with cruel pain
To do you service.
THESEUS.
I will hear that play;
For never anything can be amiss
When simpleness and duty tender it.
Go, bring them in: and take your places, ladies.
[Exit Philostrate.]
HIPPOLYTA.
I love not to see wretchedness o'ercharged,
And duty in his service perishing.
THESEUS.
Why, gentle sweet, you shall see no such thing.
HIPPOLYTA.
He says they can do nothing in this kind.
THESEUS.
The kinder we, to give them thanks for nothing.
Our sport shall be to take what they mistake:
And what poor duty cannot do, noble respect
Takes it in might, not merit.
Where I have come, great clerks have purposed
To greet me with premeditated welcomes;
Where I have seen them shiver and look pale,
Make periods in the midst of sentences,
Throttle their practis'd accent in their fears,
And, in conclusion, dumbly have broke off,
Not paying me a welcome. Trust me, sweet,
Out of this silence yet I pick'd a welcome;
And in the modesty of fearful duty
I read as much as from the rattling tongue
Of saucy and audacious eloquence.

Love, therefore, and tongue-tied simplicity
In least speak most to my capacity.
Enter Philostrate.
PHILOSTRATE.
So please your grace, the Prologue is address'd.
THESEUS.
Let him approach.
Flourish of trumpets. Enter the Prologue.
PROLOGUE
If we offend, it is with our good will.
That you should think, we come not to offend,
But with good will. To show our simple skill,
That is the true beginning of our end.
Consider then, we come but in despite.
We do not come, as minding to content you,
Our true intent is. All for your delight
We are not here. That you should here repent you,
The actors are at hand, and, by their show,
You shall know all that you are like to know.
THESEUS.
This fellow doth not stand upon points.
LYSANDER.
He hath rid his prologue like a rough colt; he knows not the stop. A good moral, my lord: it is not enough to speak, but to speak true.
HIPPOLYTA.
Indeed he hath played on this prologue like a child on a recorder; a sound, but not in government.
THESEUS.
His speech was like a tangled chain; nothing impaired, but all disordered. Who is next?
Enter Pyramus and Thisbe, Wall, Moonshine and Lion as in dumb show.
PROLOGUE
Gentles, perchance you wonder at this show;
But wonder on, till truth make all things plain.
This man is Pyramus, if you would know;

This beauteous lady Thisbe is certain.
This man, with lime and rough-cast, doth present
Wall, that vile wall which did these lovers sunder;
And through Wall's chink, poor souls, they are content
To whisper, at the which let no man wonder.
This man, with lantern, dog, and bush of thorn,
Presenteth Moonshine, for, if you will know,
By moonshine did these lovers think no scorn
To meet at Ninus' tomb, there, there to woo.
This grisly beast (which Lion hight by name)
The trusty Thisbe, coming first by night,
Did scare away, or rather did affright;
And as she fled, her mantle she did fall;
Which Lion vile with bloody mouth did stain.
Anon comes Pyramus, sweet youth, and tall,
And finds his trusty Thisbe's mantle slain;
Whereat with blade, with bloody blameful blade,
He bravely broach'd his boiling bloody breast;
And Thisbe, tarrying in mulberry shade,
His dagger drew, and died. For all the rest,
Let Lion, Moonshine, Wall, and lovers twain,
At large discourse while here they do remain.
[Exeunt Prologue, Pyramus, Thisbe, Lion and Moonshine.]
THESEUS.
I wonder if the lion be to speak.
DEMETRIUS.
No wonder, my lord. One lion may, when many asses do.
WALL.
In this same interlude it doth befall
That I, one Snout by name, present a wall:
And such a wall as I would have you think
That had in it a crannied hole or chink,
Through which the lovers, Pyramus and Thisbe,
Did whisper often very secretly.
This loam, this rough-cast, and this stone, doth show

That I am that same wall; the truth is so:
And this the cranny is, right and sinister,
Through which the fearful lovers are to whisper.
THESEUS.
Would you desire lime and hair to speak better?
DEMETRIUS.
It is the wittiest partition that ever I heard discourse, my lord.
THESEUS.
Pyramus draws near the wall; silence.
Enter Pyramus.
PYRAMUS.
O grim-look'd night! O night with hue so black!
O night, which ever art when day is not!
O night, O night, alack, alack, alack,
I fear my Thisbe's promise is forgot!
And thou, O wall, O sweet, O lovely wall,
That stand'st between her father's ground and mine;
Thou wall, O wall, O sweet and lovely wall,
Show me thy chink, to blink through with mine eyne.
[Wall holds up his fingers.]
Thanks, courteous wall: Jove shield thee well for this!
But what see I? No Thisbe do I see.
O wicked wall, through whom I see no bliss,
Curs'd be thy stones for thus deceiving me!
THESEUS.
The wall, methinks, being sensible, should curse again.
PYRAMUS.
No, in truth, sir, he should not. 'Deceiving me' is Thisbe's cue: she is to enter now, and I am to spy her through the wall. You shall see it will fall pat as I told you. Yonder she comes.
Enter Thisbe.
THISBE.
O wall, full often hast thou heard my moans,
For parting my fair Pyramus and me.

My cherry lips have often kiss'd thy stones,
Thy stones with lime and hair knit up in thee.
PYRAMUS.
I see a voice; now will I to the chink,
To spy an I can hear my Thisbe's face.
Thisbe?
THISBE.
My love thou art, my love I think.
PYRAMUS.
Think what thou wilt, I am thy lover's grace;
And like Limander am I trusty still.
THISBE.
And I like Helen, till the fates me kill.
PYRAMUS.
Not Shafalus to Procrus was so true.
THISBE.
As Shafalus to Procrus, I to you.
PYRAMUS.
O kiss me through the hole of this vile wall.
THISBE.
I kiss the wall's hole, not your lips at all.
PYRAMUS.
Wilt thou at Ninny's tomb meet me straightway?
THISBE.
'Tide life, 'tide death, I come without delay.
WALL.
Thus have I, Wall, my part discharged so;
And, being done, thus Wall away doth go.
[Exeunt Wall, Pyramus and Thisbe.]
THESEUS.
Now is the mural down between the two neighbours.
DEMETRIUS.
No remedy, my lord, when walls are so wilful to hear without warning.
HIPPOLYTA.
This is the silliest stuff that ever I heard.

THESEUS.
The best in this kind are but shadows; and the worst are no worse, if imagination amend them.
HIPPOLYTA.
It must be your imagination then, and not theirs.
THESEUS.
If we imagine no worse of them than they of themselves, they may pass for excellent men. Here come two noble beasts in, a man and a lion.
Enter Lion and Moonshine.
LION.
You, ladies, you, whose gentle hearts do fear
The smallest monstrous mouse that creeps on floor,
May now, perchance, both quake and tremble here,
When lion rough in wildest rage doth roar.
Then know that I, one Snug the joiner, am
A lion fell, nor else no lion's dam;
For if I should as lion come in strife
Into this place, 'twere pity on my life.
THESEUS.
A very gentle beast, and of a good conscience.
DEMETRIUS.
The very best at a beast, my lord, that e'er I saw.
LYSANDER.
This lion is a very fox for his valour.
THESEUS.
True; and a goose for his discretion.
DEMETRIUS.
Not so, my lord, for his valour cannot carry his discretion, and the fox carries the goose.
THESEUS.
His discretion, I am sure, cannot carry his valour; for the goose carries not the fox. It is well; leave it to his discretion, and let us listen to the moon.
MOONSHINE.
This lanthorn doth the hornèd moon present.

DEMETRIUS.
He should have worn the horns on his head.
THESEUS.
He is no crescent, and his horns are invisible within the circumference.
MOONSHINE.
This lanthorn doth the hornèd moon present;
Myself the man i' the moon do seem to be.
THESEUS.
This is the greatest error of all the rest; the man should be put into the lantern. How is it else the man i' the moon?
DEMETRIUS.
He dares not come there for the candle, for you see, it is already in snuff.
HIPPOLYTA.
I am aweary of this moon. Would he would change!
THESEUS.
It appears by his small light of discretion that he is in the wane; but yet, in courtesy, in all reason, we must stay the time.
LYSANDER.
Proceed, Moon.
MOON.
All that I have to say, is to tell you that the lantern is the moon; I the man i' the moon; this thorn-bush my thorn-bush; and this dog my dog.
DEMETRIUS.
Why, all these should be in the lantern, for all these are in the moon. But silence; here comes Thisbe.
Enter Thisbe.
THISBE.
This is old Ninny's tomb. Where is my love?
LION.
Oh!
[The Lion roars, Thisbe runs off.]
DEMETRIUS.
Well roared, Lion.
THESEUS.
Well run, Thisbe.

HIPPOLYTA.
Well shone, Moon. Truly, the moon shines with a good grace.
[The Lion tears Thisbe's mantle, and exit.]
THESEUS.
Well moused, Lion.
DEMETRIUS.
And then came Pyramus.
LYSANDER.
And so the lion vanished.
Enter Pyramus.
PYRAMUS.
Sweet Moon, I thank thee for thy sunny beams;
I thank thee, Moon, for shining now so bright;
For, by thy gracious golden, glittering gleams,
I trust to take of truest Thisbe sight.
    But stay! O spite!
    But mark, poor knight,
  What dreadful dole is here!
    Eyes, do you see?
    How can it be?
  O dainty duck! O dear!
    Thy mantle good,
    What, stained with blood?
  Approach, ye Furies fell!
    O Fates, come, come;
    Cut thread and thrum;
  Quail, rush, conclude, and quell!
THESEUS.
This passion, and the death of a dear friend, would go near to make a man look sad.
HIPPOLYTA.
Beshrew my heart, but I pity the man.
PYRAMUS.
O wherefore, Nature, didst thou lions frame,
Since lion vile hath here deflower'd my dear?

Which is—no, no—which was the fairest dame
That liv'd, that lov'd, that lik'd, that look'd with cheer.
Come, tears, confound!
Out, sword, and wound
The pap of Pyramus;
Ay, that left pap,
Where heart doth hop:
Thus die I, thus, thus, thus.
Now am I dead,
Now am I fled;
My soul is in the sky.
Tongue, lose thy light!
Moon, take thy flight!
Now die, die, die, die, die.
[Dies. Exit Moonshine.]

DEMETRIUS.
No die, but an ace, for him; for he is but one.

LYSANDER.
Less than an ace, man; for he is dead, he is nothing.

THESEUS.
With the help of a surgeon he might yet recover and prove an ass.

HIPPOLYTA.
How chance Moonshine is gone before Thisbe comes back and finds her lover?

THESEUS.
She will find him by starlight.
Enter Thisbe.
Here she comes, and her passion ends the play.

HIPPOLYTA.
Methinks she should not use a long one for such a Pyramus. I hope she will be brief.

DEMETRIUS.
A mote will turn the balance, which Pyramus, which Thisbe, is the better: he for a man, God warrant us; she for a woman, God bless us!

LYSANDER.
She hath spied him already with those sweet eyes.
DEMETRIUS.
And thus she means, videlicet—
THISBE.

Asleep, my love?
What, dead, my dove?
O Pyramus, arise,
Speak, speak. Quite dumb?
Dead, dead? A tomb
Must cover thy sweet eyes.
These lily lips,
This cherry nose,
These yellow cowslip cheeks,
Are gone, are gone!
Lovers, make moan;
His eyes were green as leeks.
O Sisters Three,
Come, come to me,
With hands as pale as milk;
Lay them in gore,
Since you have shore
With shears his thread of silk.
Tongue, not a word:
Come, trusty sword,
Come, blade, my breast imbrue;
And farewell, friends.
Thus Thisbe ends.
Adieu, adieu, adieu.

[Dies.]
THESEUS.
Moonshine and Lion are left to bury the dead.
DEMETRIUS.
Ay, and Wall too.

BOTTOM.
No, I assure you; the wall is down that parted their fathers. Will it please you to see the epilogue, or to hear a Bergomask dance between two of our company?
THESEUS.
No epilogue, I pray you; for your play needs no excuse. Never excuse; for when the players are all dead there need none to be blamed. Marry, if he that writ it had played Pyramus, and hanged himself in Thisbe's garter, it would have been a fine tragedy; and so it is, truly; and very notably discharged. But come, your Bergomask; let your epilogue alone.
[Here a dance of Clowns.]
The iron tongue of midnight hath told twelve.
Lovers, to bed; 'tis almost fairy time.
I fear we shall outsleep the coming morn
As much as we this night have overwatch'd.
This palpable-gross play hath well beguil'd
The heavy gait of night. Sweet friends, to bed.
A fortnight hold we this solemnity
In nightly revels and new jollity.
[Exeunt.]
Enter Puck.
PUCK.
Now the hungry lion roars,
And the wolf behowls the moon;
Whilst the heavy ploughman snores,
All with weary task fordone.
Now the wasted brands do glow,
Whilst the screech-owl, screeching loud,
Puts the wretch that lies in woe
In remembrance of a shroud.
Now it is the time of night
That the graves, all gaping wide,
Every one lets forth his sprite,
In the church-way paths to glide.
And we fairies, that do run

By the triple Hecate's team
From the presence of the sun,
Following darkness like a dream,
Now are frolic; not a mouse
Shall disturb this hallow'd house.
I am sent with broom before,
To sweep the dust behind the door.

Enter Oberon and Titania with their Train.

OBERON.

Through the house give glimmering light,
By the dead and drowsy fire.
Every elf and fairy sprite
Hop as light as bird from brier,
And this ditty after me,
Sing and dance it trippingly.

TITANIA.

First rehearse your song by rote,
To each word a warbling note;
Hand in hand, with fairy grace,
Will we sing, and bless this place.

[Song and Dance.]

OBERON.

Now, until the break of day,
Through this house each fairy stray.
To the best bride-bed will we,
Which by us shall blessèd be;
And the issue there create
Ever shall be fortunate.
So shall all the couples three
Ever true in loving be;
And the blots of Nature's hand
Shall not in their issue stand:
Never mole, hare-lip, nor scar,
Nor mark prodigious, such as are
Despised in nativity,

Shall upon their children be.
With this field-dew consecrate,
Every fairy take his gait,
And each several chamber bless,
Through this palace, with sweet peace;
And the owner of it blest.
Ever shall it in safety rest,
Trip away. Make no stay;
Meet me all by break of day.

[Exeunt Oberon, Titania and Train.]

PUCK.

If we shadows have offended,
Think but this, and all is mended,
That you have but slumber'd here
While these visions did appear.
And this weak and idle theme,
No more yielding but a dream,
Gentles, do not reprehend.
If you pardon, we will mend.
And, as I am an honest Puck,
If we have unearnèd luck
Now to 'scape the serpent's tongue,
We will make amends ere long;
Else the Puck a liar call.
So, good night unto you all.
Give me your hands, if we be friends,
And Robin shall restore amends.

[Exit.]

Thank you for your purchasing the book!

"I hope you enjoyed your reading. To improve our work, please write us a review and share your thoughts with us. Your support is greatly appreciated!"

Printed in France by Amazon
Brétigny-sur-Orge, FR

19849701R00050